# Little Faith

# Little Faith

## or

# The Child of the Toy Stall

## by

# Mrs. O. F. Walton

This editon © copyright 2000
Reprinted 2003
Christian Focus Publications
ISBN: 1-85792-567-X

Published by
Christian Focus Publications Ltd
Geanies House, Fearn,Tain, Ross-shire,
IV20 1TW, Scotland, Great Britain.
www.christianfocus.com
email: info@christianfocus.com

Originally published by Lutterworth Press

Printed and Bound in Great Britain by
Cox & Wyman

Cover Illustration by Albert Anker

# Contents

## The Toy Stall

It was market day, and everyone in that busy town was even busier than usual.

The marketplace was crowded with people of all ages and occupations, hurrying along as if every moment was of consequence to them, and pushing and jostling against everyone else, as if it were quite impossible that any one's business could be of as much importance as theirs.

It was a curious old marketplace; not a large open square, with plenty of room to move about between the various stalls, as in most of our more modern towns, but a long, narrow, old-fashioned street, with a row of stalls on each side of the road, close to the pavement, and only just room enough between the rows for the carts and carriages to pass through.

All sorts of things might be bought at these little stalls. There was the cap stall, with innumerable caps of all sizes and shapes - caps for old men, caps for young men, caps for big boys, caps for little boys, and caps for baby boys.

There was the stocking stall, where were displayed, in tempting rows, blue stockings, white stockings, grey stockings, brown stockings, black stockings, and striped stockings. There was the bootlace stall, with its hundreds of bootlaces, hanging side by side on strings which were stretched from one side of the stall to the other. There was the basket stall, at which you could buy a clothes-basket, a market-basket, a fish-basket, a cap-basket, a fruit-basket, or a dinner-basket. There was the sweet stall, which was always surrounded by children, who seemed to be trying to devour its contents by means of their greedy glances.

There was the gingerbread stall, which was hardly less popular, with its rows of gingerbread cats with pink eyes, gingerbread dogs with blue eyes, and gingerbread men with no eyes at all. There was the picture stall, which was a favourite resort for young men and women who were setting up housekeeping, containing a number of pictures of ladies and gentlemen dressed in every colour of the rainbow, and surrounded by most brilliant and startling frames.

And then there were the numberless toy stalls, standing side by side, and all of them very much alike.

At one of these stood a man and a child, watching the faces of the people as they passed by, and holding up one thing after another from the stall to tempt them to buy. The man was tall and thin, and one of his coat sleeves hung empty at his side, for he had lost his right arm.

The child had an anxious, thoughtful face, and looked older than her years. She was not more than ten years old, though she might have been taken for twelve or thirteen.

Crowds of people passed the stall, but no one stopped to buy. A few turned over the things, asked their price, and then walked on again, and did the same at the next stall. The man seemed very anxious to secure a purchaser, and was very clever in trying to suit the tastes of the various passers-by. The old men and women were invited to stop to examine the quality and cheapness of a pipe or a spectacle case. The mothers of families were pressed to take "just a pretty penny toy or two to the bairns at home"; the young girls were invited to buy the long strings of yellow and blue beads which were hanging across the top of the stall, and which could be made into necklaces, or bracelets, or chains, according to taste; the young men were shown cheap knives, cheap pocket-combs, cheap breast-pins, and cheap shirt-studs; whilst the children were called, again and again, to look at the trumpets, the dolls, the tops, the balls, and the boxes of toys with which the stall abounded.

But none of them fell into the traps so carefully laid for them. No one seemed to want anything that Friday morning; the little girl tinkled the penny bells to show how well they sounded, and made Jack jump out of his box again and again, but all in vain! A child came and bought a halfpenny slate-pencil, but not another halfpenny did they take the whole morning.

"Bad luck, today, Faith," said the man, as they sat down on a box behind the stall to eat their scanty dinner.

"Oh, maybe it will be a bit better this afternoon," said the child; "the country folk don't care about carrying a lot of things about with them all day - we tend to make more in the afternoons than mornings."

"We never make a great deal at any time," said the man, gloomily, as he got up to show off his wares again.

The afternoon was cold and wet. The rain came down in torrents, and Faith shivered as she wrapped her thin, faded shawl round her which was becoming more drenched every moment.

"Here, Faith, child," said the man, putting a piece of sacking around her, "keep thyself warm, bairn; I can hold on as long as thou art well."

It seemed of very little use their stopping in the market-place. The people who passed along were hurrying on to get shelter from the rain, and scarcely glanced at the stall as they went by.

The country people had all gone home, and the market-place was becoming very empty. The owners of the cap stall, of the basket stall, and of the bootlace stall were hastily packing up their wares and preparing to depart.

But still the man and the child held on. The toys were not getting wet - that was one good thing. The covering of the stall was waterproof, and there was no wind. So hour after hour they waited, hoping to the last that customers might come to the stall.

It was quite dark now, and the few stall keepers who remained had lit their lights and hung them up under cover of their stalls. The passers-by became few and far between as the night went on. At last the great church clock over their heads struck eleven, and the market-keeper came to see the lights put out and the street cleared.

The man and the child packed up the unsold articles in their various cases without saying a single word to each other, and put out their lights. Then the man put the boxes on a hand-cart, and took them to a house nearby, where a friend of his lived, who took charge of them till the next market day.

The child was white and tired. and seemed as downcast as the man. He gave her his hand when all was stored away, and then they walked on towards their home.

The streets were very quiet now, for it was half-past eleven, and they met very few people on their way. They had gone down several streets before either of them spoke. The man was the first to break the silence.

"Only sixpence the whole day, Faith," he said. "We never had such bad luck as that before!"

"What will Mrs. Gubbins say?" said the child.

"Ay!" he said; "what will Mrs. Gubbins say? Well, well, we can't help it, we've done our best, anyhow."

But he was evidently as much afraid of Mrs. Gubbins' displeasure as she was.

At last they stopped at a door in a dirty, miserable street. The door was unbolted, so the man went in, and Faith followed him up a long rickety staircase, which seemed as if it would give way beneath their weight.

They passed two landings, and then they reached a door at the top of the high house. The man paused for a moment, as if he were almost afraid to enter.

"Can't be helped," he said, almost with a groan, as he went in. The child followed him with a timid, shrinking step.

It was a dirty, forlorn room. The floor was rough and uneven, and full of holes, and the rotten boards creaked and strained as they walked across them. The walls were damp and discoloured, and covered with filth; the little window had not a whole pane to boast of, but was patched up with rags and newspaper.

There was hardly any furniture in the room, only a small round table, two or three broken boxes, and one dilapidated armchair. In this chair, with her feet on the fender and her hands stretched out over the fire, sat an old woman. Her back was turned to the door, and she never looked round as the man and the child came in.

Faith crept quietly past her to a corner of the room where three children lay asleep under a dirty blanket. They slept with their clothes on, unwashed, uncombed, and uncared for. They had no mother.

"Oh! If she could see them!" said Faith to herself as she stooped down to kiss a little grimy, sticky hand which was peeping out from a corner of the dirty blanket.

"Oh! If she could only see them, what ever would she say! It's to be hoped folks in heaven don't know what goes on."

The man sat down on a box by the table, and leaned his head on his hand. There was a strong smell of gin in the room; the old woman had been having her supper just before they came in.

"Well," she said, without turning round, "the same old tale, I suppose?"

"Yes," he said, "we've been very unlucky today, Mrs. Gubbins, very unlucky!"

"Unlucky! You always are unlucky," said the woman, bitterly.

"Can't help it," said the man, as he tossed the sixpence across the table; "that's every penny I got, Mrs. Gubbins, every penny."

"You ought to be ashamed of yourself, John Robinson," said the old woman, turning round and glaring at him with her bloodshot eyes; "you ought to be ashamed of yourself, taking the bread out of your own bairns' mouths and a-giving of it to them as hasn't no sort of a claim upon you!"

"Not a word of that, mother," said the man; "it's of no use you saying aught about that: haven't I told you so afore?"

"But I will say summat about it," said Mrs. Gubbins, "and I say it's a sin and a shame, it is; and what's more, I won't have it, I won't."

"Hold your tongue," said the man, angrily, as he heard the sound of a little stifled sob from the corner of the room; "my Mary loved that bairn, and I'm not a-going to let her go."

"We'll see about that," said Mrs. Gubbins. "I'll have a word with the parish officer when I sees him next. What's the good of the House, I should like to know, if bairns who haven't got anybody to look to 'em can't go there? I'll manage it, John Robinson, don't you be bothering your head about it."

"But I tell you she shan't go!" said John, as he smote the table angrily. "I'll see you go first ."

"Will you indeed?" said the woman, scornfully, as she covered herself with an old shawl, and laid down to sleep; "I'd like to see you, I would."

The man sat quite still, till the sound of her loud snoring broke the silence of the room. Then he crept to the corner where the children were sleeping. Faith was still awake, her hands were over her face, and she was crying quietly.

He bent over her and whispered softly: -

"Don't take on so, little Faith; don't take no notice of her; they shan't never take you away from me, bless you! Don't, don't cry, little Faith!"

The child felt his hand on her hair, stroking it very gently, and she felt something warm and wet fall on her hand! Could it be a tear?

## Faith's Flight

Yes, it was a tear, and it was not the only tear which John Robinson shed that night. He loved little Faith dearly, quite as much as if she had been his own child. Her poor mother had died in the next attic when Faith was three weeks old. Her husband had deserted her some time before the baby was born, so that when she was gone the poor little thing was left alone in the world. John's wife, Mary, had brought it into their room, crying, cold and hungry. She had comforted it, warmed it, and fed it, and they had never had the heart to turn it out again.

"Let her bide," Mary had said; "she'll maybe bring a blessing with her, poor bairn!"

And little Faith had been nothing but a blessing ever since - at least so John

Robinson thought. She had always loved him, and always been a comfort to him. It was a year now since Mary had died, and Faith had been his little comforter ever since.

But what was to be done with the children whilst he and Faith were out on market days? That was the question to be decided when his wife died. And, in an evil moment, he had accepted the offer of his wife's mother, Mrs. Gubbins, to come and live with him, and to look after the little ones. He would never have had her if he had known what she was. But she lived in a town many miles away, and neither he nor poor Mary had seen her for many years. So when her letter came, in which she offered to come and live with him, he was very pleased, and thought it was a way out of his difficulty.

And Mrs. Gubbins came, and, having come, she stayed.

And in less than a week, his clean, comfortable room was changed into a pigsty; the children became neglected and disorderly, and all the quiet and peace and rest dropped out of his life.

But John Robinson was a weak man, and he became thoroughly afraid of Mrs. Gubbins. He had not the courage to send her away, and from day to day he endured in silence. He was oppressed and unhappy; he longed to turn her out, and dared not.

But tonight she had roused his anger as never before. Send little Faith away! He would never allow her to do that! No, as soon as she woke he would order her out, and have his room in peace again. John Robinson fell asleep.

But Faith was also making a resolution, and she did not go to sleep. She lay awake, listening intently to every sound in the room. Mrs. Gubbins was snoring loudly, and, after a time, John Robinson followed her example.

Faith listened a long time to be quite sure he was asleep; then she crept from under the blanket and stood upright on the floor. The boards creaked as she did this and she stood perfectly still for some moments, so that she might be sure that the noise had not awakened either the man or the old woman. But the snoring went on as before; so Faith stooped down very, very quietly, and then she groped her way to the door.

It was quite dark, for the fire had gone out, and John Robinson had put out the candle before he went to sleep and she was very much afraid of stumbling over Mrs.

Gubbins, who was lying somewhere in front of the fire.

Slowly and cautiously, and yet trembling so much that she could hardly stand, she felt her way to the door.

Oh, how the boards creaked and strained. Little Faith shook with fear!

But no one moved in the room. They did not hear the noise. John Robinson was tired out with his hard day's work, and Mrs. Gubbins was heavy with drink. It would have taken a much louder noise than little Faith's quiet footstep to have wakened either of them.

So Faith reached the door, quietly unlatched it, and crept out.

Then she began to descend the long, rickety staircase. And this was a work of time, for it was almost impossible not to make some noise here, so rotten and broken were the boards. Oh, how thankful she felt when she had passed both the landings, and no one had heard her! And now she cautiously unbolted the street door, and looked out.

It was a pitch-dark night; not a star was in the sky. The rain was falling fast and, by the light of the one dingy gas light in the street, Faith could see that the road and pavement were covered with pools of water and mud. It was a dark, dismal, dreary night.

Little Faith was about to shut the door behind her and venture out into the darkness when she heard a footstep coming down the street. It was a man's footstep, and he was stumbling along as if he were drunk. Then he began to scream and shout, and Faith drew back into the house and shut the door before he came up. She dared not venture into the darkness alone. She had heard that bad people were about at night; what if she should meet any of them?

No, she dared not go till the morning. She would sit on the stairs till it was light.

So she crept back again, and sat on the lowest step, and leaned her head on her hands. The wind blew through the draughty old house and underneath the badly fitting door, and made her shiver as she sat there. She was very cold, and very sad, and very tired.

But little Faith had a Friend. Yes, lonely and desolate as she was, she had a Friend to whom she could turn. He had been her Friend for a long time now, and as she sat there, alone in the darkness, she whispered softly to herself some words which Mother Mary, as she always called Mrs. Robinson, had taught her: -

What a Friend we have in Jesus,
All our sins and griefs to bear;
What a privilege to carry
Everything to God in prayer!

Oh, what peace we often forfeit!
Oh, what needless pain we bear!
All because we do not carry
Everything to God in prayer.

Have we trials and temptations?
Is there trouble anywhere?
We should never be discouraged, -
Take it to the Lord in prayer.

Can we find a friend so faithful,
Who will all our sorrows share?
Jesus knows our every weakness, -
Take it to the Lord in prayer.

"Yes," she said, when she had finished the hymn, "I've never told Him anything about this trouble. Whatever will He think of me?"

So she knelt down on the step and said in a whisper, "God, I want to tell you, please, all about it. Mrs. Gubbins says I'm taking the bread out of the bairns' mouths, so please I'm a-going away, and will you help me to find somebody who wants a little servant? And will you please take care of Tommy, and Fanny, and the baby, and don't let Mrs. Gubbins slap 'em, for Jesus Christ's sake. Amen."

Then Faith got up, and felt much happier. She knew her Friend would help her. She had carried it all to the Lord in prayer, and now she must not fret about it anymore. "That was what Mother Mary used to say," said Faith to herself. "She told me I was to take all my troubles to the Lord and then leave 'em with Him, and not bother about 'em no more. She said it was a sin and a shame to doubt Him, and to think He wouldn't give us anything, if we asked Him, and it was good for us."

So little Faith tried to forget her sorrow; and by and by she fell asleep.

How long she slept she did not know,

but when she awoke the grey morning light was creeping under the door, and peeping through the keyhole, and making the dirty, dusty walls of the old staircase visible once more.

Faith started up and opened the door, and then went out into the rain and mud.

It was still quite early, and she had gone down several streets, and felt as if she were a long way from home before the church clock struck five. The streets were almost empty. No one passed her except a solitary policemen, a doctor returning from a patient who had sent for him in the night and a workman whose work lay at a great distance from his home.

But presently, as time went on, and it got near six o'clock, the streets were nearly filled with working men, in their white jackets, hurrying along to their work.

Then shutters began to be opened and fires to be lighted, and smoke to come out of the chimneys.

Still Faith walked on. She wanted to get to quite a different part of that large town, where nobody knew her, and where she would never meet Mrs. Gubbins. She was very faint and hungry, for she had had no supper the night before. She had one penny in her pocket, which Mother Mary had given her long ago, and which she had kept for her sake. Faith had almost thought of giving it to her father, as she called John Robinson, the night before, when he was so unhappy about having taken so little money. But it would not have made much difference, and she was glad now that she had kept it, for it would buy her some breakfast. And then she must begin to look for a little place where she could be a servant.

But, first, she must make herself tidy. No one would take an untidy little girl, she thought. For this purpose she went down an alley, where there was a pump in the middle of the square, and washed her hands and her face.

Then she took a comb from her pocket, which had belonged to the stall, but which her father had given her the day before, because it was broken, and could not be sold. With this she combed her hair, and plaited it neatly up again.

Mary Robinson had taught her to be very clean and tidy, and her little frock, though it was full of patches and darns, had not a single hole in it. Since Mother Mary had died, Faith had mended it for herself. She looked a very clean, tidy child when she came out of the alley, and set out in search of a shop at which to spend her penny.

She found a baker's shop at last, but it was not open; the baker and his family had overslept. Faith was thinking of going on to look for another shop. But she turned so faint and sick that she was obliged to sit down on the baker's step. She felt she could walk no further until she had had something to eat.

At last the door was opened, and a boy came out and took down the shutters. Then Faith walked into the shop.

"Well, what's wanted?" said the baker's daughter, as Faith held out the penny.

"Please," said Faith, in a faint voice, "I want the biggest cake you've got for a halfpenny."

"You look half hungered," said the girl, as she handed her a tea-cake. "Sit on that chair and eat it. Mother, come here!" she called, in a louder voice.

A fat, rosy, good-tempered looking woman answered the call.

"She wanted the biggest cake we've got for a halfpenny," said the girl. "Look at her; she's half starved!"

"Where are you off to?" said the baker's

wife to Faith, as she sat eating her cake.

"Please, ma'am," said little Faith, "I'm looking for a place. I'm going to be a servant somewhere. Do you know of anybody who wants a little girl?"

"Why, now," said the woman to her daughter, "doesn't Miss Benson want one?"

"Ay," said the girl, "so they say; but maybe she wouldn't take such as her."

"There's no harm in asking. Take the child across to her, Maggie."

So Faith followed Maggie across the road; but, before she went, the good baker's wife gave her two more large tea-cakes, and gave her the halfpenny back again which her daughter had taken.

"Jesus made her do that, I'm sure," said Faith to herself.

Miss Benson was not up, and they had to wait some time to see her, and then when she did come downstairs she seemed quite angry with Faith for coming, and with the baker's daughter for having brought her.

"Want a servant? Yes, she did want a servant; but a proper, respectable sort of servant, not a little, weakly, sickly child. She should have thought they would have known that, without needing to be told"; and, so saying, she showed them out.

The baker's daughter took a kind leave of the child, but said she was afraid she did not know of anyone else.

So little Faith went on alone, very sorrowfully.

### Faith's Search

Up and down the streets, up and down the streets, hour after hour, little Faith wandered, first asking at one shop and then at another. Sometimes she would venture to stop the passers-by, and inquire of them. She would choose someone whose face looked kind and motherly, and put the same question again and again: "Could you tell me of anyone who wants a little servant, please?"

But she got nothing but discouragement the whole day long. One told her she was too small; another that she was too delicate; another brought tears to her eyes by telling her to go home to her mother; one or two laughed at her, and not a few were angry with her. And so the day wore away.

It was getting near evening, and was beginning to grow dark. Faith had asked her question hopefully and eagerly in the morning; but now she asked it in quite a different voice, and as if she hardly expected an encouraging answer. She was very tired, sad, and disappointed. Her Friend had not helped her, she thought. She had taken it to the Lord in prayer, but no answer had come. Mother Mary had said it was wicked to doubt; but how could she help doubting when God did not seem to hear her?

She was very footsore and tired, so she sat down on a doorstep to rest. She wondered what Mrs. Gubbins had said when she found she was gone; and whether her father missed her - she wondered if he was looking for her all over that great town.

And then Faith remembered that it was Saturday night, and that her father would be at his place at the stall. She wondered how far the marketplace was from where she was sitting. She had a great longing just to see her father for a minute. She did not want him to see her - that would never do. No, she would never go home again till she had found a little place, and was earning money for herself. But what she wanted was to try to get a peep at her father, to see if he looked sorrowful, or tired, or as if he was missing her very much.

Faith got up from the doorstep, and asked a girl who was passing the way to the marketplace. The girl directed her, and to Faith's joy she found it was close by.

In a few minutes she came in sight of the great church underneath the shadow of which stood John Robinson's stall.

The street was very crowded; there was always a very full market on Saturday night. People were buying in their stores for the week, and were going in and out of the different shops in the marketplace, with large baskets on their arms. All was bustle, hurry, and confusion.

Faith threaded her way through the crowd, and went down a little side street which led into the marketplace, and which ran along the side of the old church. She crept along close to the railings of the church, till she came nearly to the end of the street; but she did not dare to go further, lest her father should see her. She could see the top of the stall from where she stood, but she could not see her father. She did not like to go round the corner, for that would have brought her close up to the stall, and he would have seen her at once.

Faith had nearly made up her mind to go back again when she noticed that the

37

church gate was open. She was almost afraid to go inside, but at last she ventured. In front of her was a porch leading into the church, and in this porch she saw that there was a window looking in the direction of the stall, through which she would be able to see her father without his seeing her. So she ran quickly across the open piece of churchyard, and got inside the porch.

Then she looked out of the window. John Robinson's stall was not more than thirty yards away. She could see him quite well, surrounded as he was by flaring oil lamps; but he could not see her at all in the darkness and shadow of the church porch.

This was just what little Faith wanted. She stood there for a long time watching him. He looked very sad, she thought, and very tired. Nobody seemed to be buying anything, and she longed to run across the road and spend her penny at the stall. If only she could be somebody else, for just one moment, and run across and buy a penny toy, that he might have one more penny to take home to Mrs. Gubbins!

What would Mrs. Gubbins say if he brought her nothing home tonight?

Well, there would be one less mouth to feed, that was a comfort. She could not blame him any more for giving the children's bread to her.

How anxiously Faith watched for customers to the stall; and how glad she was when at last an old man stopped and bought one of the best sixpenny pipes!

But her father did not seem half as glad as she thought he would have been. He put the money in his pocket, but he did not look a bit pleased. He did not seem to be thinking much about it. All the time the old man was there, all the time he was showing off his wares, all the time he was waiting for purchasers, he was gazing up and down the street, first this way and then that way, as if he was looking for someone.

"Can he be looking for me?" said Faith to herself. "Oh, I hope he doesn't miss me too much! P'raps I shouldn't have run away, but ought to have stopped with him, and cheered him up. But I did it all for him. Mrs. Gubbins goes on at him so about me! Oh, dear, oh dear; I hope he isn't very unhappy!"

There was a low stone seat on each side of the church porch, and Faith sat down on this, and hid her face in her hands and cried. She was very tired and disheartened. Once she thought she would go out, and go back to her father, but then she did not dare to go back to Mrs. Gubbins again till she had found work for herself. No, she could not do that.

But night was coming on, and where would she sleep? She would be very frightened indeed if she had to be out alone in the street all night!

What could she do? Should she pray again? She thought she would. Perhaps if she asked the Lord Jesus again to help her He would hear her. She could not understand why He had not heard her before. It was very strange. But she would try once more. She would tell Him how tired and lonely she was, and how much she was afraid of being out in the street all night. Perhaps when He saw how very unhappy she was He would tell her where to go.

Faith was just going to kneel down when she heard the sound of singing inside the church. She put her ear to the door and listened.

Faith thought she had never heard such a beautiful tune. She opened the door just a crack, that she might, if possible, hear the words, and then she peeped in.

To her astonishment she could not see anyone in the church. One or two of the gas lamps were lighted, and she could see the great stone pillars, and the high arches, and long aisles of the old church, but she could not see a single man or woman or child. There were a great many pews, but they were all empty; and there was a high pulpit, but there was no one standing in it. She opened the door a little wider and went in. There did not seem to be anyone in the old church but herself.

Where could the singing have come from?

Faith walked a few steps farther into the church, and then she stopped again. She felt rather afraid at the sound of her feet upon the stone pavement.

The singing had stopped, but presently she heard the voice of someone reading aloud. The voice seemed to come from the other side of the church. After waiting for some minutes, Faith walked on tip-toe in that direction. She wanted very much to know where the sound came from.

Presently she saw a door in that part of the church open, and an old man looked out to see who was walking about in the church. He caught sight of Faith, and came towards her. She felt very much inclined to run away; she was afraid he would be angry with her for coming into the church.

But the old man did not look cross or vexed, but smiled at her as he came up, so Faith decided not to run away.

When the old man was close to her he asked her, in a whisper, what she wanted.

"Please sir," said Faith, "I wanted to hear 'em sing; they was singing so beautifully when I was outside there - but I couldn't find anybody!"

"They're all in the vestry," said the old verger; "it's prayer meeting night. It's always prayer meeting ona Saturday night. You'll have to sit very still if I let you come in."

"Will they let me come in?" said Faith, in a faltering voice; "won't they be cross if I go?"

"Oh, no," said the man, "not if I take you, bairn, and if you are a good girl. Come along; you can sit on the seat by me." So he gave Faith his hand, and took her into the vestry.

The vestry was nearly full. There were about thirty people present, sitting in rows, and the minister was standing in front of them, reading a chapter out of the Bible. Then they knelt down and prayed.

Little Faith was very tired and sleepy. She

sat in the corner by the old verger, and he kept nodding kindly to her; but the warmth and comfort of the room, after her bad night, and after the cold and fatigue of the day, made her eyes very heavy.

Presently, as the minister was reading again, she fell asleep.

She had not been asleep more than a minute or two when she was wakened up suddenly by hearing her own name. She had been dreaming of Mother Mary, and thought she was sitting beside Mother Mary's bed, as she had done for so many days and nights before she died, and then she thought someone asked her a question, and this question awoke her: -

"Little Faith, wherefore didst thou doubt?"

She started up and opened her eyes, but Mother Mary was not there! Faith found herself in the vestry, on the seat beside the old man; and he looked very surprised to see her jump up so suddenly.

And yet she felt quite sure that she had really heard a voice asking her that question. Yes, and she felt quite sure that it was the same voice which was reading now! It was the minister who had said: -

## "Little Faith, wherefore didst thou doubt?"

How could he know about her?

Who could have told him that her name was little Faith?

How did he know that she had been praying, and had not got an answer to her prayer, and was beginning to doubt?

Jesus must have told him; she felt sure of that. Nobody else knew.

The minister did not say anything else about her. She listened very attentively now, but he did not mention her name again. He was reading about a ship, and the wind ceasing, and the ship getting to land.

It was very strange that he should have stopped in the middle to speak to her!

But little Faith felt she had got a message from Heaven. Jesus must have told him to ask her that question. He was very sorry she had doubted Him, and told the minister to tell her so.

Faith said to herself that she would never doubt any more. She was quite sure now that she would have an answer to her prayer very soon indeed.

Her Friend had heard her after all, and

was going to help her. She felt quite glad and happy, and as if a great weight had been taken off her heart.

## A Happy Sunday

The prayer was over, the blessing was given, and the people rose to leave.

But little Faith still sat on. The old verger came up to her, and told her kindly that it was all done now, and she had better be thinking of going home, as it was getting late, and he was going to lock the church up.

"Please, sir," said little Faith, "do you think the minister would let me speak to him?"

"Ay, to be sure," said the old man; "wait a minute and I'll ask him."

The minister was talking to an old lady, who had stopped behind the rest to tell him of someone who was ill, and wanted to see him. As soon as she had done speaking, the verger went up to him, and, pointing to

Faith, said, "Here's a little girl who has been sitting by me in the meeting, and wants to speak to you, sir."

The minister called Faith to him, and asked her what she wanted.

"Please, sir," she said, "I won't ever do it again."

"You won't do what, my child?" said the minister.

"I won't ever doubt Him again," said Faith. "It was very wrong, I know it was - Mother Mary said so; but I won't do it anymore, I won't. Did He tell you to speak to me, and to ask me that?"

The minister looked very puzzled.

"What does she mean, Barnes?" he said to the old verger. "When did I speak to her, and ask her anything? I cannot remember that I ever saw her before."

"Please, sir," said Faith, "it was just now when I was sitting there by him. I was very tired with walking about all day, and I was very nigh asleep, and then I heard you calling of me, and asking that."

"I think you must have been dreaming, dear child," said the minister; "I never asked you anything."

"Didn't you?" said little Faith, in a very disappointed voice. "Oh! I thought it was you; it must have been a dream then!"

"What was it, dear?" said the old lady, who had been putting on her cloak whilst they were talking. "What did you think Mr. Barker asked you?"

"Please ma'am." said Faith, with tears in her eyes, "I heard somebody saying to me, 'Little Faith, wherefore didst thou doubt?' and I thought it was the minister, and that Jesus had told him what they called me, and all about me."

"Oh, I see now," said the minister kindly; "Is your name Faith?"

"Yes, sir, Faith Emmerson."

"It was in the chapter I read tonight," said Mr. Barker to the old lady. "Don't you remember that Jesus said to Peter, 'O thou of little faith, wherefore didst thou doubt?'"

"Yes! Of course," said the old lady, "that was it. Poor child! Wasn't it strange?"

"Then Jesus didn't tell you about me, after all?" said the child.

"No," said Mr. Barker, "He did not tell me about you; but I am sure, if you have been doubting Him, little Faith, that He has sent you here that I might ask you that question. I am quite sure He meant it for you. Now will you not tell me why you have been doubting Him? What was it about?"

Little Faith burst into tears, "Oh, please," she said, "Mrs. Gubbins says I'm taking the bread out of the children's mouths, so I've run away to be a little servant; and nobody wants me. I walked about all day asking of people, and there isn't anybody who wants me. I've asked at all the little shops, and none of them wants a girl just now; and I've asked the folks in the street, and none of them wanted anybody neither. There isn't anybody who wants me! And before I started I asked Jesus to help me, and He hasn't helped me a bit yet, and now I don't know whatever I shall do tonight!"

"Now," said the minister, "I want to hear all about it. Sit down on the seat beside me, and tell me. And first, who is Mrs. Gubbins?"

Little Faith sat down beside the minister, and little by little he got from her her history. When she had told him all, and he understood quite well what she wanted, he turned to the old lady, who was waiting and listening also, and asked her advice as to what was to be done.

"Don't you think you had better go home to your father tonight, Faith, and stop with him till I hear of work for you?" said the old lady.

"Oh, please no!," said Faith. "I don't ever want to go back to Mrs. Gubbins. What would she say? She'd probably be ever so angry with me. Oh, please don't send me back till I can tell them I've got a little place!"

"Well, Mr. Barker," said the old lady, after thinking for a minute or two, "I'll take little Faith home with me tonight. She may stop with me till Monday, and then we can talk about it again, and see what can be done."

"That is indeed good of you, Mrs. Fraser," said the minister. "Little Faith, Jesus has heard your prayer, you see, and has sent this kind lady to help you."

Little Faith was smiling very happily now, poor child; she felt as if the burden had been rolled away from her.

They went out of the vestry, and walked through the old church, where Barnes was busy putting out the gas-lights. Then they came to the church porch, and Faith could see her father. He was still standing behind the stall, holding up his wares to the passers-by.

"Please, ma'am," said Faith to the old lady, "that's my father."

"Had not we better go and tell him, Faith?" she said.

"No, please not," said little Faith, "not

till I've got a little place; please don't tell him now."

So when they got to the gate the old lady and Faith went the other way round the church. The minister said, "Good-night," for he was going to see the sick person of whom Mrs. Fraser had told him.

Mrs. Fraser took hold of Faith's hand, and they went on down several streets till they came to the old lady's house. They stopped at the door, and Mrs. Fraser rang the bell. It was not at all a large house, but it looked very grand and beautiful to little Faith. There was a small bay window on one side of the door. The venetian blinds were down, but not closed, and the flickering of the firelight within looked very comfortable and inviting.

The door was opened by a clean and tidy servant, in a white apron and cap.

"Now, Ellen," said her mistress, "I've brought this little girl to spend Sunday here. Will you give her some tea, and take care of her? Now, Faith, go with Ellen. I am sure you will be happy with her."

Faith followed Ellen into the cosy little kitchen, where there was a blazing fire; and Ellen told her to sit down on a stool in front of the fire, whilst she got her mistress's supper ready.

Faith sat still, and watched Ellen moving about the kitchen, quickly and yet quietly, and setting out the supper tray very neatly and prettily; and she wondered if ever she would be so clever, and be able to be of so much use as a servant.

Then the tray was carried into the room, and Ellen came back to attend to Faith. She made the child take off her wet frock, and she brought down a warm jacket of her own for Faith to wear till her frock was dry. And then she gave her such a supper as Faith had not had for many a day, certainly not since Mother Mary died. The food and the hot coffee brought a colour into her pale cheeks, and Ellen declared she looked "a sight better now".

Faith was very glad to go to bed, and slept very soundly after her long, tiring day.

The next day was Sunday, and what a happy Sunday it was for Faith! She went with Ellen into the old church, and sat beside her, and heard the minister preach and the people sing; and she thought it must be very like that in heaven where Mother Mary was.

Then after tea she and Ellen went into the dining room to old Mrs. Fraser, and they read a chapter together in the Bible, and the old lady talked to them about it. Faith could read a little; she had always gone to school when Mother Mary was alive, except on market days, and then her father had heard her read to him as they sat together on the box behind the stall. Faith was very pleased to be allowed to read her verse in turn.

Mrs. Fraser chose the chapter which the minister had read at the prayer meeting on Saturday night, and in which came the question which Faith had heard as she woke up from sleep: "O thou of little faith, wherefore didst thou doubt?"

"Do you love the Lord Jesus, little Faith?" said Mrs. Fraser, when she had done reading.

"Yes, ma'am," said little Faith, "ever so much, I do."

"Why do you love Him, Faith?" asked the old lady.

"Please, ma'am, because He died for me. Mother Mary said I couldn't go to heaven if Jesus hadn't died for me. She said God would have had to punish me for being naughty so often, and couldn't ever have taken me to live in His beautiful home, if Jesus hadn't been punished instead of me. It was good of Him, wasn't it?"

"I am so glad you know that," said the

old lady, "because we have no right to call God our Friend, little Faith, till we have come to Jesus as our Saviour.  Many people talk about God helping them, and being merciful to them, and yet all the time they never come to God through Jesus, never take Jesus for their own Saviour.  But you have done that;  haven't you, little Faith?"

"Yes, please, ma'am,"  said little Faith. Mother Mary taught me a hymn, to say when I said my prayers of a night and morning.  It begins:

*Just as I am - without one plea,*
*But that Thy blood was shed for me,*
*And that Thou bidst me come to Thee,*
*O Lamb of God, I come.*

"And I try to come every time I say it."

"Dear child,"  said Mrs. Fraser.  "I am so glad of that.  And now, little Faith, I am sure you have a Friend in Jesus, and so you must never doubt Him, little Faith.  'Wherefore didst thou doubt?'  Don't forget that question;  it grieves Him so if you doubt Him."

"Yes,"  said little Faith,  "Mother Mary said so."

"Just think, Faith," said the old lady, "after I've tried to be kind to you, and taken you in here, and am trying to make you happy, and am ready to do anything I can for you, if you were to doubt me and to say: 'I don't think Mrs. Fraser will give me any breakfast tomorrow,' or 'I don't think Mrs. Fraser will really look out for a place for me,' or 'I don't believe this,' or 'I'm so afraid of that.' Why, little Faith, what should I think of you?"

Little Faith laughed.

"I would never do that," she said.

"No, little Faith," said the old lady, "you wouldn't doubt me; then do you think you ought to doubt the Lord Jesus, who has done so much more for you than I have done?"

"No," said Faith, "I must never do it again."

Then Mrs. Fraser knelt down, and prayed that she and Ellen and Faith might always trust their Heavenly Friend, and never doubt his love, but that every time they felt tempted to do so, they might hear His tender, loving voice saying to them as He did to Peter, "O thou of little faith, wherefore didst thou doubt?"

## The Empty Place

It was Friday morning, and little Faith was going to the market to see her father. She had waited until Friday that she might be able to see him at the stall, for she did not want to go home to meet Mrs. Gubbins.

Faith had so much to tell her father that he would be pleased to hear. The minister and Mrs. Fraser had had a long talk about her on Tuesday evening. It had been settled that they should get her father's consent for her to stop in Mrs. Fraser's house for six months, that the old lady and Ellen might teach her and train her to be a useful little servant, and then the minister and Mrs. Fraser very kindly promised to find a nice situation for her, where she might earn money for herself. Oh, how glad her father would be when he heard this good news!

Faith dressed herself very tidily, in the pretty pink frock which Mrs. Fraser and Ellen had made for her, and put on her new brown hat, trimmed so prettily and so neatly with brown velvet.

"I wonder if father will know me?" said Faith to herself, as she looked in the looking glass before starting. "Maybe he'll think it's somebody else. He'll never think it's me, as smart as this! Oh dear, how pleased he'll be!"

It was quite early when Faith started for the marketplace, not more than nine o'clock. She was so happy that Friday morning that she hardly knew what she was doing. She had helped Ellen to get the breakfast ready, but she had spilled the milk and let the kettle boil over, and had let one of the silver spoons fall. She had had so many mishaps in various ways, that Ellen had laughed at her, and had told her that she had better get her breakfast and go at once, for it was clear she was too excited to do anything else.

So now Faith was ready to go. She ran quickly downstairs, and in the hall she found Mrs. Fraser.

"Well, little Faith," said the old lady, "tell your father I will take great care of you - and take this with you to spend at the stall. You would like to buy something, I know." And Mrs. Fraser put a florin in the child's hand, and told her that she might buy anything she pleased with it.

Two shillings to spend at her father's stall!

If Faith had been in good spirits before, she was almost wild now. Two shillings! What a number of things that would buy! And her father, how pleased he would be! No one had ever spent two shillings at the stall before. Mrs. Gubbins would be almost in a good temper if he took so much money home to her at night.

What could she buy? She thought she would get a nice present for Ellen, who had been so kind to her. What should it be? She turned over in her mind all the contents of the stall, but could not fix upon anything. No, she must wait until she got there, and talk it over with her father.

Oh, how surprised he would be when she appeared, and how glad and thankful when he heard how happy she was, and how good God had been to her! Faith felt as if her feet would not go fast enough. It seemed such a long time since she had seen her father, and it was almost like a dream to think of speaking to him again, and telling him of all that had happened to her during that strange week.

At last the old church came in sight, and Faith turned down the little side street, that she might come out just in front of her father's stall. She was getting very near now; she could see the basket stall and the cap stall, which were just at the end of the street. Another moment and she would be there! Oh, how little Faith's heart beat as she hurried on!

She turned the corner - and then she suddenly stood still - rooted to the spot in amazement and dismay. Her father was not there! The stocking stall, the gingerbread stall, the bootlace stall, and all the other toy stalls were going on as usual, but her father's place was empty.

Little Faith was so disappointed that she burst into tears.

What could be the reason? Where could her father be? Had he changed his place? She wandered a little way down the marketplace to see, but no - that was not likely, for she had often heard him say that he liked this place at the corner of the two streets better than any in the marketplace.

And then, too, her father's place was empty. No other stall had been moved there.

What could be the matter? She was sure that no small reason would keep him away from the stall. She could only remember one market day when he had not been there, and that was the day Mother Mary had died. That sorrowful day! It was very fresh in little Faith's memory still. She remembered how they had sat by her bed, and her father was holding her hand, and she had said, "You won't go today, John"; and he had said, "No, dear, of course I won't." And then he had sat there, holding her hand, till she had gone away from them to heaven.

Little Faith had thought of all this now, as she sat down on the coping stone of the church railings wondering what had become of her father. What could be the matter?

Was one of the children dead? Had Mrs. Gubbins been getting drunk, and let them fall into the fire or down the stairs? Little Faith had always been afraid of that, and had always charged Tommy, the eldest one, to take care of the others whilst she was out. Could it be that? It made her shudder to think of it!

Perhaps her father was ill - very, very ill, like Mother Mary had been, with no one to nurse him, or love him, or look after him? It was a dreadful thought, and the tears ran down the child's face as her mind dwelt upon it.

Suddenly it occurred to her that she should ask the other stall keepers if they had seen anything of her father. So she went up to Tom Jenkins, the owner of the basket stall, and asked him if he had seen her father in the marketplace that morning.

"Why, bless me!" said Jenkins, looking very closely at her, "is it little Faith?"

"Yes," said Faith, "it's me. I've got a little place; I came to tell father about it, and he's gone."

"Well," said Jenkins, "I can't think, for the life of me, what's got him. He was here on Tuesday, only half the day, though; but he hasn't been here today."

"Did he look ill?" said little Faith.

"Aye," said Jenkins, "very downhearted, he was. I don't know what was wrong with him. I said to my mate there, when we went home at night, 'There must be something amiss with Robinson.' But he never said anything about it to any of us."

"What can it be?" said little Faith.

"I don't know, my lass, I'm sure," said the basket man, as he turned away to show off his wares to some country people who were passing the stall; "maybe that man will know," and he pointed to the cap stall proprietor, who was standing idly behind his stall with his hands in his pockets.

Faith went to him, but he couldn't give her any information whatsoever. She asked at one or two of the other stalls, but with the same result. No one could throw the least light on the reason for her father's absence. There was nothing to be done but to go back and tell Mrs. Fraser.

So with a heavy heart Faith turned back. How slowly she walked homewards, so differently from the way in which she had come down to the marketplace. She even turned round once or twice, and looked at the empty place again, as if it could not possibly be anything but a dream that her father's stall had vanished from the place where it had stood for so long.

When Faith got to the house Ellen let her in, and was beginning to ask her, in a cheerful voice, if her father knew her, when she noticed how sad and downcast the child looked.

"Where is Mrs. Fraser?" said little Faith, as she began to cry again.

"She's here in the diningroom," said Ellen, kindly. "Come in and speak to her."

She opened the door, and Faith went in, and, holding out the florin, she sobbed out, "Please, ma'am, he's gone; he isn't there! I can't find him anywhere! None of the stall keepers have seen him today. Oh dear, whatever shall I do?"

Mrs. Fraser made Faith sit down beside her, and talked it over with her for a long time; and at last it was decided that, after dinner, Faith should go to her old home to see what was the matter there.

Faith did not eat much dinner that day; she was very anxious and very troubled. She did not forget, before she started, to go into the little bedroom which she shared with Ellen, and, kneeling down, to take her trouble to the Lord in prayer, and to ask her Heavenly Friend to go with her. For she could not help dreading meeting Mrs. Gubbins again, and she did not know in what trouble or sorrow she might find her father.

As she went down the well-known streets, and got nearer and nearer to Belfry Row, she kept asking again and again for help for whatever was before her.

At last little Faith reached the house, and quietly opened the door. And then she stood still, and felt almost afraid to go farther.

What would Mrs. Gubbins say when she

went in? All Faith's dread of the old woman returned upon her.

She crept cautiously and quietly up the rickety stairs. The house was very noisy as usual; the two landings were full of screaming, quarrelling children, and bad and angry words were heard on all sides. Faith had never noticed how wretched the house looked before. When she had lived there she was so accustomed to the noise and dirt and the misery that she had hardly seen it.

But now, when she had come from Mrs. Fraser's beautiful house, where everything was so clean and comfortable, Faith wondered how she could ever have been happy in Belfry Row. It looked so very forlorn and wretched, she thought.

The people on the two landings took no notice of her as she passed by. John Robinson's family had kept very much to themselves, and did not know any of the other people in the house. There was no one now living on the same floor with them, and those below seemed as far away as if they lived in another house, for they never saw them except when they passed by their rooms as they went down to the street door, and they did not even know their names.

The people of the house were constantly changing. Nearly every week fresh ones came, and so, even if they had wished to get to know them, it would have been very difficult. So Faith passed by, and no one stopped her or noticed her.

At last she reached the top landing, and there before her was the well-known door. She waited for a minute or two, wondering what she should do, and then she knocked.

No one came to open the door, and Faith could not hear any sound inside the room.

Surely the children could not be asleep yet; it was only four o'clock. The church clock in the street struck as she stood at the door.

Faith knocked again, and waited again, but she got no answer. "They must be all out," she thought; "I expect the door is locked; I shall have to come again." She wondered where they could have gone; they had never all been out together since Mother Mary died.

Faith thought she would try the door before she went away; perhaps Mrs. Gubbins had been looking out of the window, and would not let her in, and was making the children sit very quiet that she might not hear them.

Faith's heart beat very fast at the thought. Should she lift the latch and go in? What would Mrs. Gubbins do? Would she knock her down as soon as she went in, and then turn her out? Not if her father was there, Faith felt sure of that. But she did not think her father could be there, unless he was very ill, or he would have opened the door.

No, they must all be out; she would just try the door, and then go away.

So Faith put her hand on the latch, and was almost startled at the sound it made going down.

The door was open, and Faith went in.

### What Faith found in the attic

Faith went into the room, but it was not empty. Her father was not there, nor the children, but in the corner of the room, in the place where the children used to sleep, Mrs. Gubbins was lying on the ground with her face turned to the wall. She did not look round as Faith went in, but lay perfectly still.

Could she be asleep, or was she only pretending to be asleep, that Faith might go away again? The child felt tempted to do this; she was so terrified at the thought of being alone there with Mrs. Gubbins. But then she remembered that it was almost tea time. Surely her father and the children would soon be in, and then she could see them before she went.

So Faith sat down on a box and waited. Mrs. Gubbins did not move or speak, and

Faith concluded that she must really be asleep. No doubt she had been drinking heavily, and had fallen on the bed to sleep the heavy sleep of drunkenness, as Faith had seen her do so often before. On the table was a black bottle and a broken cup. The bottle had no cork in it, and was lying on its side. There was a strong smell of spirits in the room, as if the old woman had knocked it over when she got up from her seat, and the contents had been spilled on the floor.

Faith sat still on the box, straining her ears for the sound of her father's footstep on the stairs; but no one came. Not a sound, except the distant noise of quarrelling and screaming children coming up from below.

The room was very cold. The fire had evidently burnt out some time since, and Faith shivered as she sat near the door. She once thought that she would go farther into the room where she would be out of the way of the draught; but she was so afraid that Mrs. Gubbins would wake and be angry with her, that she thought she would keep close to the door, that she might make her escape as soon as the old woman moved.

Time passed on, and still no one came. What could they be doing? Where could her father have taken them?

The church clock struck five. It was getting dark now. Faith could only dimly see the form of Mrs. Gubbins stretched in the corner of the attic. She did not know what to do. Mrs. Fraser would be expecting her at home, and would wonder that she had stayed so long, yet she could not bear the thought of not seeing her father after all. Was there no one who could tell her anything about him? No, she could not think of anyone. The people downstairs were newcomers, and probably did not know anything whatever of the inhabitants of the attic. There was no one but Mrs. Gubbins. Should she wake her and ask her, or should she go away without hearing of her father.

Faith decided to go away; but when she was halfway down the stairs she changed her mind. It would be terrible to wait till tomorrow to know what was the matter with her father. All night long she would be wondering where he was, and she would lie awake thinking of him, she was sure of that. For a very dreadful thought had crossed her mind. Was her father dead, and had Mrs. Gubbins sent the children to the workhouse? The more Faith thought of this the more she felt afraid that this was what was the matter. She could not go home without knowing the truth. So she went back again and knocked once more, very loudly, at the attic door. She hoped that Mrs. Gubbins would awake, and come to the door, and then she could speak to her there without going inside.

But no sound was to be heard within, though Faith repeated her knock three or four times. So she opened the door and went into the attic again. Mrs. Gubbins was lying just as Faith had seen her before; she did not seem to have moved at all.

"I shall have to speak to her," said the child to herself. "She seems so very sound asleep."

She crossed the rotten floor, trembling at the noise she made, and went up to where Mrs. Gubbins was lying.

Then Faith stood still for a minute, and prayed. She took it to the Lord in prayer. She asked her Friend to stand by her, and help her, and not to let Mrs. Gubbins hurt her.

As she prayed, she happened to look up at the skylight window, and there, looking down into the dark dismal attic, was a bright and beautiful star. Little Faith looked at the star, and it seemed to be smiling at her, she thought. It seemed like the loving eye of the Lord Jesus watching her, and she thought she heard Him asking her that question again, "Little Faith, wherefore didst thou doubt?"

Oh, what strength it gave her! Faith felt that her prayer was heard. Jesus was by her side, and He would help her. She would be no longer afraid.

"Mrs. Gubbins!" said Faith, in a whisper. "Mrs. Gubbins!"

But Mrs. Gubbins did not hear.

"Mrs. Gubbins! Mrs. Gubbins!" she repeated, much louder than before.

But no answer came.

"Mrs. Gubbins! Mrs. Gubbins!" She almost shouted the words this time; but still the old woman did not move. "How very sound asleep she must be!" thought the child.

It was nearly dark now, so that Faith could only just see Mrs. Gubbins' face, but she fancied that her eyes were not quite closed. One hand was hanging out from under the blanket close to Faith, and the child took hold of it, thinking that she would in this way be able to rouse the old woman from her heavy sleep.

But she had no sooner taken Mrs. Gubbins' hand than she started back in terror. The hand was icy cold. Faith had never felt anything like it since Mother Mary died. She remembered how she had crept to Mother Mary's side the night after she died, not liking to go to sleep without giving her a kiss as usual, and then she remembered how startled she had been to find her so very, very cold, for she had never seen death before. Now Mrs. Gubbins' hand felt like that, cold and motionless. Could Mrs. Gubbins be dead? Faith ran to the door, and down the stairs as fast as she could.

"What is it? What's the matter?" said a woman who was coming out of her room on the next landing, and heard Faith's footstep, and saw by the light of her candle how pale and frightened the child looked.

"Oh, please," said little Faith, "I wish you'd come upstairs; I believe she's dead!"

"Dead! Who's dead?" said the woman. "What is it, child? Tell me who's dead?"

"Mrs. Gubbins!" said Faith, "the old woman who lives upstairs. Haven't you ever seen her passing by?"

"What? That old woman who is always going out for drink? Ay, I've seen her," said the woman.

Two or three more women came out of their rooms at this moment, and they all agreed to go upstairs with Faith.

The woman with the candle went first, and flashed the light on the old woman's face.

"Yes, she's gone," she said, solemnly; "she's gone, poor thing! Dear me, has she nobody belonging to her?"

Faith told them in a few words who she was, and asked them if they could tell her anything of her father and the children. One woman told her that they had left the house together last Tuesday afternoon, and had never been seen since; but where they had gone no one knew. Another woman said Mrs. Gubbins had been backwards and forwards several times the day before with a bottle in her hand, but none of them had seen her at all today.

Then they talked together about what was to be done. The news had by this time spread all over the house and throughout Belfry Row, and quite a crowd of people filled the little attic - mothers with babies in their arms, troops of noisy, dirty children, and one or two idle and ragged men.

There was much talking and many exclamations of horror. After each person had separately related when he or she had last seen Mrs. Gubbins, and their feelings of horror and surprise when they had been summoned to the attic just now, and told that she was dead - they came to the conclusion that Jem Payne, one of their number, should go at once to the parish officer and report the case to him, and leave the matter in his hands.

When all this was settled Faith turned to go; she was glad to leave the attic and to go homewards. She felt very awe-struck and solemn as she walked home, and yet she could hardly realise it. Mrs. Gubbins is dead! Alone in the attic, dead! And her father gone she knew not where! It all seemed too strange and too dreadful to be true.

Faith was very glad when she reached Mrs. Fraser's house, and was able to tell the kind old lady all that had happened.

"Oh, Faith!" said Mrs. Fraser, when she had heard it all, and they were talking it over together, "May God keep you, my dear child, from the love of drink! It is a terrible thing when a man drinks, but oh, I think it is worse when a woman drinks!"

"Mrs. Gubbins didn't always drink so bad," said Faith; "but she got worse and worse lately."

"Yes," said Mrs. Fraser, "people always get worse and worse. Satan tempts them, and then they yield, and then he tempts them again, and they yield again, and he gets a greater hold on them every time. Only God's grace, little Faith, can enable a drunkard to lose his love of drink; nothing else will do it. Pledges alone cannot do it; resolutions alone cannot do it; nothing but God's grace helping him can keep him from falling. Does your father drink, little Faith?"

"Oh, no," said Faith, "*never* - not a drop, he doesn't. He always brought every penny he took home to Mother Mary, and then, when she was dead, to Mrs. Gubbins. Oh, poor father, I wonder where he is!"

"Do you remember that verse, Faith," said Mrs. Fraser, "'If ye shall ask anything in My name, I will do it'?"

The child thought she had heard it before, but she did not know it perfectly, so Mrs. Fraser found it for her in her New Testament, and made her learn it. "Now, little Faith," she said, when the child had repeated the verse correctly, "God knows where your father is. He sees him at this moment, just as you see me. He sees what he is doing, and what the children are doing. He knows the name of the place they are in, and the name of the street, and the number of the house. He knows all about them, whether they are ill or well, or in want or comfort. Now, little Faith, you would like very much to know about all this too, wouldn't you?"

"Oh, yes," said little Faith, "that I should, ma'am!"

"Very well," said Mrs. Fraser, "then we will kneel down and ask God to tell you, and then, if it is good for you to know, I am quite sure, little Faith, that in some way or other He will help you. Can you believe that, little Faith?"

"Yes," said the child, "I think I can."

So Mrs. Fraser and Faith knelt down together.

It was a very simple prayer, so simple that Faith could understand every word of it. Mrs. Fraser took all the trouble to the Lord in prayer, telling Him the sorrow of little Faith's heart, and how she longed to know where her father was, and asking Him, if He saw it would be good for her to let her know.

"Now, Faith," said Mrs. Fraser, when they rose from their knees, "having done this you must leave the matter with God, who knows best. Do not trouble about it any more, because, if you do that, you will show plainly that you do not trust Him. Go about your work patiently, and, whenever you are tempted to be sorrowful, you must think that you hear the Lord Jesus saying to you, 'O thou of little faith, wherefore didst thou doubt?' If you only trust Him, really trust Him, an answer will come. I am sure of that."

Little Faith wiped away her tears, and went downstairs with a bright and cheerful face. She had taken her trouble to the Lord in prayer, and she had left it with Him.

Now she had nothing to do but to wait patiently for the answer.

## Found at last

It is never easy to be patient, and as days and weeks and even months went by, and Faith heard nothing of her father, sometimes her faith failed her. She wondered if, after all, God would answer her prayer. But Mrs. Fraser always cheered her, and encouraged her, and told her she must be willing to wait God's time.

The child was very happy in Mrs. Fraser's house, and day by day she was becoming more useful as a servant. Ellen had great pleasure in teaching her to do all kinds of housework, and in training her in habits of neatness and order.

The six months during which Mrs. Fraser had promised to keep her were almost ended, but the old lady did not seem at all inclined to look out for a situation for Faith.

She told the minister that the child was too young to go amongst strangers and to do hard work, and that she would like to keep her in her own house, to pay her wages, and to train her until she was older and stronger. Faith was very thankful when she heard of this kind offer, for she was quite sure that she would never be so happy anywhere as she was in Mrs. Fraser's house; all went on so peacefully and happily there from day to day. The mistress was thoughtful and considerate for the comfort of her servants, and the servants loved their kind mistress, and would not have grieved her for the world. Every morning and night they prayed together, and took their wants, and sins, and sorrows, to the Lord in prayer.

Ellen found in Faith a very willing little helper in her work. She never idled away her time, but did her work cheerfully and well. When she was sent on an errand she went as quickly as she could, and never stopped to talk or gossip on the way.

One bright September morning, just six months after Faith had come to live with Mrs. Fraser, Ellen sent her to a shop at some little distance from home to buy something that was needed for dinner.

It so happened that in order to get to

this shop, Faith had to pass down the marketplace. It was so strange to see everything there looking just the same as it did in the days when she and her father used to stand behind the toy stall three times a week. The country people were hurrying past as usual; the sweets stall and the gingerbread stall were still surrounded by children; the stocking man, the bootlace man, and the basket man were still loudly calling to the passers-by to come and examine their wares.

Faith stopped for a moment before the place where her father's stall had stood. A new toy stall was there in its place, and a man was standing behind it, and his little girl was helping him to sell his goods, just as she had always helped her father.

"I wonder if they have taken much today?" said Faith to herself.

The little girl looked pale and tired, she thought, and the man did not seem to be in very good spirits.

Faith had sixpence of her own in her pocket, and she determined to spend it at the stall. Perhaps they would be as glad as she and her father would have been on one of those long, tiring days which now seemed so far away. So she went up to the stall and bought a new sixpenny comb.

The little girl smiled, and seemed so pleased to get the sixpence that Faith went on with a light and happy heart.

She had nearly passed the old church when she heard someone calling her, and looking round, she saw the owner of the basket stall waving his arms, and heard him calling "Faith!" at the top of his voice. She ran to him at once to see what he wanted.

"Here, my lass," said the man, "have you ever heard anything of your father?"

"No," said little Faith, "not a word."

"Well," said he, "my Matty said that she saw him go by the other day."

"Oh, where?" cried little Faith, "Where did she see him? Was it here?"

"Oh, no," said the man, as he wiped his eyes with the back of his hand. "Matty won't never come here no more; you remember Matty, don't you?"

"Is she your little girl that used to come with you?" said Faith.

"Ay," he said, "the same; but she's very badly now; she'll never come no more, so the doctor says!"

"I'm so sorry," said little Faith. "Would you mind telling me where she saw my father?"

"She saw him pass the window. I was out at the stall, but when I came in, 'Father,' she says, 'I saw the toy stall man, who used to be next to us, go by today; he must live somewhere here.' She never forgets folks' faces, does Matty. Go and see her; she'll tell you all about it."

He told Faith where he lived, and then she hurried on to make up for lost time.

Was her prayer really going to be answered at last? It was a very happy thought, and it was with a very bright face that she carried the good news to Mrs. Fraser. The old lady was very glad to hear it, though she told Faith not to be too sure that by this means she should find her father, but to believe that even if it did not come now, still God's answer to her prayer would not stop away a single day after God's time came.

That afternoon Mrs. Fraser gave Faith leave to go to Trundle Street, where little Matty lived, that she might hear all that the child could tell her.

It was a dark, dismal street, full of high houses, let off in rooms, and was very much like Belfry Row, Faith's old home. The room to which the basket man had directed her was on the ground floor, on the left hand side of the door.

Faith knocked gently, and a voice within said: "Come in; they are all out but me."

So Faith opened the door and went in. It was a low, dark room, and, at first, Faith could hardly see who or what was in it. There was not much furniture, but the room was almost filled with baskets of various sizes and shapes and colours, so that there was very little space to move about in it.

On a bed, close to the window, a little girl was lying. She was propped up with pillows, so that she could see what was passing in the street. She was about Faith's age, or a little older, but she was so very thin and small that Faith could easily have carried her. When the door was first opened she coughed very much, and seemed in much pain.

"Why, it's Faith," she said, as soon as she could get her breath. "I remember you at the stall. How did you know where we lived?"

"Your father told me," said Faith. "He said you had seen my father go by, and I wanted to hear about it, because I can't find him anywhere."

"Yes," said Matty; "it was yesterday that he went by; he's never been past before, because I see everyone that goes by from the window. He had a breakfast tin in his hand, and it was just about seven o'clock in the evening."

"Are you quite sure?" said little Faith.

"Yes, quite sure," said Matty, "as sure as sure can be. There aren't many men who have only got one arm, and I know his face so well, too."

"I wonder if he'll come again?" said Faith, trembling with excitement. "If he does, Matty, do you think you could rap at the window, and stop him and tell him where I live, and how much I want to find him?"

"Ay! I'll do that," said Matty. "It's nice to be able to do anything for anyone."

"Yes," said little Faith; "it must be dreadful to lie still all day. Are you always alone, Matty?"

"Yes, till father comes in," she said. "But I tidy the room up, and make it all nice before he goes. He puts everything ready for me on this little table close beside me, and Mrs. Evans, who lives upstairs, comes in sometimes. She is very good; she boils my kettle on her fire."

"But you must be very lonely," said Faith.

"Oh, not so very lonely," said Matty. "I've got my books;" and she pulled out two or three well-read books from under her pillow; "and then you know, Faith," she added in a lower tone, "Jesus never goes away."

"Do you love Him?" asked little Faith.

"Yes," said Matty, "very much; but I didn't love Him before I was ill. I was in Miss Carter's class in the Sunday school, and oh how she did talk to us about coming to Jesus, and loving Jesus, and I never listened much; but when I was ill, then I thought about it all. Miss Carter often comes to see me, and lends me such beautiful books, and she talks to me so nice when she comes."

"Will you never be any better?" asked Faith.

"Never any better till I die," said Matty; "I shall be quite well then. Miss Carter found me the verses; I'll read you them. I put a marker in the places. This is the first; it's in Isaiah: 'And the inhabitants' (that means the people that live in heaven) 'shall not say, I am sick: the people that dwell therein shall be forgiven their iniquity.' Miss Carter says that last bit is the best part of all. And here's the other; it's in Revelation: 'There shall be no more death, neither sorrow, nor crying, neither shall there be any more pain.' Isn't that a good thing?"

"Yes, very," said Faith. "How soon do you think you'll go there, Matty?"

"I don't know," said the child; "the doctor didn't say. I would like to go very soon. I should like to go today, only there's father. Poor father! He has got nobody but me; whatever will he do when I go away?" and Matty began to cry.

"I expect Jesus will come and take care of him," said Faith.

"Yes," said Matty, "I hope so. That's why I want father so much to love Jesus; and, do you know, I think he does love Him a little, Faith. Sometimes at night he reads to me out of my Testament, and he likes me to talk about it now; and oh, I do pray for him so very often."

"Then the answer is sure to come," said Faith; "Mrs. Fraser always says so. I keep on praying to find my father, and sometimes I think I never shall find him, but she tells me I must wait God's time."

It was a lovely September evening, the sun was beginning to set, and the attic windows of the high houses opposite looked as if they were on fire, as the bright golden sunlight fell upon them.

Suddenly, as they were speaking, Matty raised herself quickly. She had been looking out of the window as they were talking, and now she gazed earnestly down the street.

"Yes," she cried, "it is he! There he is, Faith, coming down the street! Run, Faith, run!"

Little Faith did not need to be told twice. In a moment she had jumped up, opened the door, and run into the street.

Had the answer really come? Was her prayer heard?

Yes, there was no doubt of it. There, coming down the street to meet her, in his working clothes, with his breakfast tin in his hand, was her father - her father whom she had lost so long.

Would he know her, or would he pass her by as if she were a stranger? Little Faith hurried on, and in another minute she was close to her father.

## A Work for Little Faith

Yes, he did know her. When Faith was close to him her father saw her. He started with surprise for a moment, and then he took her up in his arms, and kissed her.

"Why, Faith, my little Faith!" he said, "I thought I should never find you again. Where have you been?"

"Why, father," said Faith, as well as she could for her tears, "where have you been? I thought I should never find you again. I've been looking for you all over."

"Come away home, Faith, and I'll tell you all about it," said her father, "I needn't be at work for another half-hour yet."

So Faith ran in with a bright face to say goodbye to Matty, and then took her father's hand, and walked with him back to his house.

The children did not know Faith at all, and they had grown very much since she had seen them last. The house was very forlorn, and the children very dirty.

"There's nobody to look to them, you see," said her father, "nobody but me, and I'm tired out by the time I get home from work. And now, little Faith, wherever in the world have you been?"

So Faith told her story, how she had heard what Mrs. Gubbins had said about taking the bread out of the children's mouths, and how she had gone to look for a little place where she could be a servant, and earn money for herself. She told him of her weary search that long, tiring day, and then how in the evening she had come to peep at him from the church porch, and how she had longed to spend her penny at the stall, that he might have one more penny to take home to Mrs. Gubbins.

Her father fairly broke down when Faith came to this part of her story.

"Bless you, bless you, child!" he said, "To think of you peeping out of the window at me! Why, if I'd only known you were there, wouldn't I have run and brought you out! I was looking for you all the time."

Then Faith went on to tell him how she

had heard the singing, and had gone into the church, and how Mrs. Fraser had taken her home. And then she gave him an account of her happy home, and how she was being trained to be a useful servant.

"But oh, father," said little Faith, "I've been praying every day to find you; and Mrs. Fraser said the answer would come. Where have you been all this long time?"

"Well, Faith," he said, "my story's soon told. I was real cut up when I heard Mrs. Gubbins say that about you, and I made up my mind I would turn her out as soon as I could in the morning. And the morning came, and I got up, and you were gone. I never was so angry in all my life, bairn. I told Mrs. Gubbins it was all her fault, and she might go; but she said no, she wasn't going, she should stay as long as she liked.

"Well, child, I didn't know what to do. I walked up and down all day, looking for you, but I couldn't find you. Then at night I had to go to my stall, and I looked up and down the street, but couldn't see nothing of you. And then I went home, and Mrs. Gubbins was worse drunk than ever, and she'd been beating the children, and they all looked so wretched without you, Faith, and I didn't know what to do. Well, on

Sunday it was the same, and Monday, too. Mrs. Gubbins would not turn out, and I couldn't get rid of her, and I was terrified of leaving her with the children when I was out. So on the Tuesday, I only went half a day to the stall, and then, after looking about for a while, I found a man at a little toy shop in a back street who wanted to buy some toys, and I sold him mine cheap, and then I sold my handcart to a man who I knew was looking out for one.

"Well, I put the money in my pocket, and went home, and Mrs. Gubbins was out. Now, I thought, is the time: Mrs. Gubbins won't go away from us, so we'll go away from her. So I gathered up the children's bits of clothes as quick as I could, and anything I could get hold of, and we were off before Mrs. Gubbins came back. I had seen in the newspaper that they wanted a man to carry parcels at a shop at Wingtown, that's six miles from here. Well, we went there, and I got taken on; but it was hard work and small pay. I stopped there till last week, though; then I heard they were advertising for night watchmen at the docks here, to go on board the steamers that are in port, and keep watch of a night. So I wrote and applied, and my master gave me a character reference, and they told me I might come. They pay me good wages, and I might be very comfortable, but there's nobody to do anything. I've got a few bits of furniture in, but all's in a muddle yet; I must get it put right next week. I don't think Mrs. Gubbins will find us out here; it's a good long way from Belfry Row."

"Oh, no," said Faith, "she'll never find you out. Don't you know Mrs. Gubbins is dead, father?"

John Robinson was very shocked to hear this. Faith gave him an account of her visit to the attic, and of the dreadful sight she had seen there. Then it was time for her father to go to his work, and for Faith to go back to her mistress.

Oh, with what a happy heart the child went home! Ellen guessed the good news by Faith's bright face, even before she had had time to speak a word. And no one was more pleased than Mrs. Fraser.

"Now, little Faith," she said, "has not God been good to you? Let us thank Him together."

So the old lady and Faith knelt down, and with very grateful hearts gave thanks to the Lord for His gracious answer to their prayers.

The next morning, Mrs. Fraser went to see the minister, and had a long talk with him about what little Faith was to do. At first Mr. Barker was very anxious that she should remain with Mrs. Fraser, where she had such a happy home and so many advantages; but when Mrs. Fraser reminded him how good John Robinson had been to the child, how he had taken her into his home and family when she was a little friendless orphan, and how he had always treated her and loved her as his own child, he agreed with the old lady that now, when her father really needed her help, and when she was old enough to be of some use to him, it was only right that Faith should do what she could to pay back, in some measure, all that her father had done for her.

When Mrs. Fraser came home she talked it over with Faith, and gave the little girl leave to go home at the end of the week, and, if her father wished it, to stay with him and take care of the house and children.

So early on Saturday morning little Faith set off for her new home, with an earnest prayer in her heart that she might indeed be a blessing there. It was about eight o'clock when she arrived there; Mrs. Fraser had let her go early, because it was Saturday, and she thought she would be able to make the house more comfortable for her father before Sunday.

When Faith arrived she was received with shouts of joy by the children. They were playing in the middle of the floor, drawing pictures with cinders, and making it, if possible, blacker than ever.

The fireplace was choked with ashes, and looked as if it had not been swept for days. The walls were covered with cobwebs and dust, for the house had been shut up for some time before they came to it, and had never been cleaned since they arrived. The table was covered with dirty cups and plates, and the floor was strewn with clothes, and pans, and brushes, and broken toys. It looked very forlorn and hopeless.

"Where's father?" said Faith to the children.

"He's asleep in bed; he gets home at seven, and then he goes to bed, and wakes up about two o'clock, and then he comes down and gets us some dinner."

"Let's make the room tidy and nice," said Faith, "before he wakes. Who'll help me?"

The children thought it was great fun to help Faith in her cleaning. She put on a large apron, and soon they were very busy.

They turned everything out of the kitchen into the yard at the back of the house, and then Faith took a long brush and swept the ceiling and walls. Then she black leaded the stove and cleaned the hearth.

The children got quite excited as the work went on, and really made themselves very useful.

Then the floor was washed, the window cleaned, the table scoured, and the chairs dusted and polished.

"It does look beautiful!" said Fanny, when their work was done, and Faith had lighted the fire and put on the kettle.

"Now about dinner," said Faith, as she looked with satisfaction at her work; "what time is it?"

Tommy ran to the corner of the street to look at the church clock, and came back to say it was only eleven. Faith had some money of her own in her pocket, so she went out and made her little purchases. She bought some pieces of meat and some vegetables to make into good soup, such as she had so often watched Ellen making, and some apples for dumplings for the children.

"Now, then," she said to them, when all was ready for dinner, "we must smarten you up a bit."

This was a more difficult business than even the house, but Faith took a large basin into the yard and washed them well, and combed and cut and brushed their hair, and made them look very different from what they had done when she came in.

"We must have a wash on Monday," said Faith, "and get your clothes clean and tidy."

There was no time to do more now; she could hear her father moving upstairs, for it was nearly two o'clock. Faith quite shook with excitement when she heard him coming downstairs.

John Robinson came into the room, and then stood still, mute with astonishment.

"Well, I never!" he said, at length. "I wouldn't have known the place! Bless me, Faith, darling, have you done it? Well, it's just like when Mary was alive!"

"I hope it will look much nicer soon, father," said Faith. "I must get the children's clothes done next week."

"You don't mean to say you're going to stay, Faith!" said her father, as he sat down to eat his nicely prepared dinner.

"Yes, father, if you'll have me," said little Faith.

"Have you, my lass," he said, "have you? Why you're my little comforter! Haven't I been longing to have you this great while? But I don't like to take you from such a good home!"

"Father," said little Faith, as she got up and kissed him, "do you think I could ever forget all you've done for me? And I want so much to show you how I love you for it."

That was the beginning of many happy days for John Robinson and his children. Faith was in every way his little comforter. She kept his house in beautiful order, and the children clean and tidy. Above all, she tried to lead him in the way to heaven.

Mrs. Fraser and Ellen often came to see her, and helped her in every way; and Faith felt that if she went to them she could always find sympathy in her troubles, and advice in her difficulties. She was also able to be a great comfort to little Matty, who lived very near them, and to help to nurse her, until she went to the city where there is no more pain.

Little Faith never forgot her text. Mr. Barker printed it for her in large and clear letters, and Mrs. Fraser gave her a frame in which to hang it.

It was put up on the walls in the kitchen, where everyone could see it. And whenever Faith was downcast, or troubled, or anxious, and whenever her prayers did not seem to be answered, she glanced up from her work at the text on the wall, and she heard her Lord once more asking her the question, "O thou of little faith, wherefore didst thou doubt?"

# Matthew Chapter 14 22-33

Straightway Jesus constrained his disciples to get into a ship, and to go before him unto the other side, while he sent the multitudes away.

And when he had sent the multitudes away, he went up into a mountain apart to pray: and when the evening was come, he was there alone.

But the ship was now in the midst of the sea, tossed with waves: for the wind was contrary.

And in the fourth watch of the night Jesus went unto them, walking on the sea, they were troubled, saying.

'It is a spirit.' and they cried out for fear.

But straightway Jesus spake unto them, saying,

'Be of good cheer; it is I; be not afraid.'

And Peter answered him and said,

'Lord, if it be thou, bid me come unto thee on the water.'

And he said,

'Come.'

And when Peter was come down out of the ship, he walked on the water, to go to Jesus.

But when he saw the wind boisterous, he was afraid; and beginning to sink, he cried, saying,

'Lord, save me.'

And immediately Jesus stretched forth his hand, and caught him, and said unto him,

'O thou of little faith, wherefore didst thou doubt?'

And when they were come into the ship, the wind ceased.

Then they that were in the ship came and worshipped him, saying, 'Of a truth thou art the Son of God.'

Have you enjoyed reading about little Faith? Do you ever finish reading a book and wish that you could carry on. Well the next section is what you need. Not only can you read about the lessons that little Faith learned throughout the book but you can also go on to read another chapter from one of the other Classic Fiction books. Further information is also given about books available from Christian Focus Publications. We hope that you will find out about more books you would like to read - if you do please contact your local Christian bookstore and they will be pleased to order them for you.

# Biblical Lessons

1. Prayer

2. Doubt

3. Trust

4. Care

5. Patience

# Biblical Lessons

**Prayer:**

The character in this story, Faith, speaks to God about her worries, fears and hopes. She prays to God in her own special way as though she were just speaking to any other person she knew. What worries do you have? What do you hope for the future? Are you fearful of what is round the corner in your life? The Bible tells you not to worry.

*'Do not worry, saying, 'What shall we eat?' or 'What shall we drink?' or 'What shall we wear?' For the pagans run after all these things, and your heavenly Father knows that you need them. But seek first his kingdom and his righteousness, and all these things will be given to you as well. Therefore do not worry about tomorrow for tomorrow will worry about itself. Each day has enough trouble of its own.'*
*Matthew 6:31-34*

We learn that prayer is an important part of life with God and that he is always willing to listen to us.

We do not have to put on a special act with God or speak in a clever way. Our Father, God, is delighted to hear us speak with him. In Matthew Chapter 6 verses 5-15 Jesus himself tells us how to pray. He tells us that we can speak to God just like a father... God is a perfect father... better than any father we might have on earth.

As we pray to God we should show respect but we shouldn't feel awkward or uncomfortable. We shouldn't think that we have to pray to God in the same way that other people pray to him. It is more important to have our heart right with God than to have good sounding words.

*'When you pray, do not keep on babbling like pagans, for they think they will be heard because of their many words. Do not be like them, for your Father knows what you need before you ask him.' Matthew 6:7-8.*

*'Do not be anxious about anything, but in everything, by prayer and petition, with thanksgiving, present your requests to God.' Philippians 4:6*

## Doubt:

*'Little faith, wherefore didst thou doubt'*
*Matthew 14:31.*

This verse is quoted a lot in this story. It is from Matthew 14:31. When little Faith hears the minister read this verse she thinks he is speaking directly to her. She soon learns that she has no reason to doubt God's plan or his care for her. God tells her not to doubt.

We must learn not to doubt God either. Whatever problems or concerns we have we can trust God to deliver us from them. We can believe that he knows the future and what is in our best interests. God will help you cope with whatever life brings.

*'Look at the birds of the air; they do not sow or reap or store away in barns, and yet your heavenly Father feeds them. Are you not much more valuable than they? Who of you by worrying can add a single hour to his life? Matthew 6:26-27*

So God commands you to

*'Stop doubting and believe.'* John 20:27

But if you still find this a problem, if you still find that you are doubting God and not trusting him just ask him to help you. God is amazing. He instructs us to believe and trust in him and when we find this difficult he is more than willing to help us. He gives us everything we need.

*'If any of you lacks wisdom, he should ask God, who gives generously to all without finding fault, and it will be given to him. But when he asks, he must believe and not doubt, because he who doubts is like a wave of the sea, blown and tossed by the wind.'* James 1: 5-6

Trust:

Faith believes in the Lord Jesus and begins to trust in God. At first everything goes well and her trust in God is very strong. However this waivers when she tries to find a job. She begins to look for a job as a maid and is disheartened when things don't go so well.

The struggles that Faith has bring her down and her trust in God falters. However her trust in her loving God grows again despite all her troubles. Faith believes that God is in control.

We too must learn to trust in God even in really hard times. David, the Psalmist wrote many songs about trusting in God. Think of a time in your life where it has been really hard to keep going. Prayer and sharing your problems with God really helps.

*He who dwells in the shelter of the Most High will rest in the shadow of the Almighty.*
*I will say of the Lord, 'He is my refuge and my fortress, my God, in whom I turst.*

*Surely he will save you from the fowler's snare and from the deadly pestilence. He will cover you with his feathers and under his wings you find refuge, his faithfulness will be your shield and rampart.*

*You will not fear the terror of the night, nor the arrow that flies by day, nor the pestilence that stalks in the darkness, nor the plague that destroys at midday....*

*If you make the Most High your dwelling - even the Lord, who is my refuge - then no harm will befall you, no disaster will come near your tent.*
*Psalm 91:1-10*

Life can often be a struggle but we should trust in God and not let our problems turn us away from our strong and loving Saviour, Jesus Christ. Every day trust that God is in control of what is going to come. There is nothing that he cannot help you with.

*Trust in the Lord with all your heart and lean not on your own understanding; in all your ways acknowledge him and he will make your paths straight.*
*Proverbs 3:5-6.*

## Care:

Faith's love and care for her adoptive family and the care shown to faith by the Christians she meets are good examples of how we too should care for the people around us. The Christians that Faith met showed real love for Faith and this really encouraged her. They didn't turn her away but instead took her in and loved her.

We too can show practical love for people we know. We can also show care for those people who have no family or friends. It is very easy to love people who are loveable. It is harder sometimes to show real caring love to people who are awkward or not very pleasant.

Jesus Christ showed love to all people. He didn't turn away from the lepers like other people did - he went up to them and touched them and cured them. He didn't say angry words to Zacchaeus the tax collector - instead he went to Zacchaeus's house for a meal. If we follow Jesus Christ we should behave like him. One of the most striking examples of Christ's care for you and me is that he died for us on the cross. He also died for us on the cross before we ever showed him any love. 'God demonstrates his own love for us in this: While we were still sinners, Christ died for us.' Romans 5:8

He is such a dependable trustworthy God. He is a caring God.

*'Cast all your cares on God for he cares for you.'*
*1 Peter 5:7.*

As his followers we should copy him just as little children copy their parents. When we believe in the name of Jesus he will change our selfish wicked hearts into living loving hearts.

*A friend loves at all times. Proverbs 17:17.*

## Patience:

Faith is eager to be reunited with her family but must learn to be patient and wait until God brings them together. In the meantime she perseveres in prayer.

We too must learn to be patient. Often we can ask God for something when we pray to him. We can ask him for something which he really wants to give us but sometimes his answer is 'Not yet.'

Do you ever make the mistake of thinking that because God hasn't given you what you wanted he wasn't listening? It can be very hard to be patient. Especially when we urgently need what we are praying for. The Bible tells us that we must wait.

*'Wait for the Lord. Be strong and take heart and wait for the Lord.' Psalm 27:14.*

Sometimes when we pray and don't receive an immediate answer we lose heart and stop praying. We must learn to keep praying to God. It is important to remember than God always answers our prayers - it's just that he doesn't always answer them in the way we want.

Being patient requires strength of mind and character. God is the best example of patience and if we find being patient difficult we can always ask him to show us how.

*'Be joyful in hope and patient in affliction.'*
*Romans 12:12.*

*'Love is patient, love is kind.' 1 Corinthians 13:4.*

*'Be patient and stand firm.' James 5:8.*

This book is reprinted by request of people who have read and enjoyed this book in the past. *Little Faith* has been edited slightly to make the book more accessible to a new generation but the editorial we believe has been in keeping with the original style of the book and does not take away from the simplicity of the story and its message. We hope that this book will enjoy many more years of popularity as a result.

## Little Faith

This is a lovely story. I really enjoyed travelling along with this little girl called Faith, through her ups and downs, her hopes and fears, her loneliness and her disappointments. I'm amazed by her simple trusting faith in God and I'm also very glad that there's a happy ending! It's just a shame that I didn't discover this book when I was a little girl - but it has been lovely all the same!

God bless you as you enjoy it too.

Marina MacRae
Publishing Assistant

If you enjoyed reading this book read the following chapter which is from 'A Peep Behind the Scenes.' This is another book written by O F Walton and published by Christian Focus Publications.

# 'A Peep Behind the Scenes.'

*Rosalie*

Rain, rain, rain! How mercilessly it fell on the fair-field that Sunday afternoon! Every moment the pools increased and the mud became thicker. How dismal it all looked! On Saturday evening it had been brilliantly lit, and the grand shows in the most aristocratic part of the field had been illuminated with crosses, stars, anchors, and all manner of devices.

But there were no lights now; there was nothing to cast a halo round the dirty, weather stained tents and the dingy caravans.

Yet, in spite of this, and in spite of the rain, a crowd of Sunday idlers lingered about the fair, looking with great interest at the half-covered whirligigs and bicycles, peeping curiously into the deserted shows, and making many schemes for further enjoyment on the morrow, when the fair was once more to be in its glory.

Inside the caravans the show people were crouching over their fires and grumbling at the weather, murmuring at having to pay so much for the ground on which their shows were erected, at a time when they would be likely to make so little profit.

A little old man, with a rosy, good-tempered face, was making his way across the sea of mud which divided the shows from each other. He was evidently no idler in the fair; he had come into it that Sunday afternoon for a definite purpose, and he did not intend to leave it until it was accomplished. After crossing an almost impassable place he climbed the steps leading to one of the caravans and knocked at the door.

It was a curious door; the upper part of it, being used as a window, was filled with glass, behind which you could see two small muslin curtains, tied up with pink ribbon. No one came to open the door when the old man knocked, and he was about to turn away, when some little boys, who were standing near, called out to him:

'Rap again, sir, rap again; there's a little

lass in there; she went in a bit since.'

'Don't you wish you was her?' said one of the little boys to the other.

'Ay!' said the little fellow, 'I wish *our* house would move about, and had little windows with white curtains and pink bows!'

The old man laughed a hearty laugh at the children's talk, and rapped again at the caravan door.

This time a face appeared between the muslin curtains and peered cautiously out. It was a very pretty little face, so pretty that the old man sighed to himself when he saw it.

Then the small head turned round, and seemed to be telling what it had seen to someone within, and asking leave to admit the visitor; for a minute afterwards the door was opened, and the owner of the pretty face stood before the old man.

She was a little girl about twelve years of age, very slender and delicate in appearance. Her hair, which was of a rich auburn colour, was hanging down to her waist, and her eyes were the most beautiful the old man thought he had ever seen.

She was very poorly dressed, and she shivered as the damp, cold air rushed in through the open door.

'Good afternoon, my little dear,' said the old man. She was just going to answer him when a violent fit of coughing from within caused her to look round, and when it was over, a weak, querulous voice said hurriedly:

'Shut the door, Rosalie; it's so cold; ask whoever it is to come in.'

The old man did not wait for a second invitation; he stepped inside the caravan, and the child closed the door.

It was a very small place. At the end of the caravan was a narrow bed something like a berth on board ship, and on it a woman was lying who was evidently very ill. She was the child's mother, the old man felt sure. She had the same beautiful eyes and sunny hair, though her face was thin and wasted.

There was not room for much furniture in the small caravan; a tiny stove, the chimney of which went through the wooden roof, a few pans, a shelf containing cups and saucers, and two boxes which served as seats, completely filled it. There was only just room for the old man to stand, and the fire was so near him that he was in danger of being scorched.

Rosalie had seated herself on one of the

boxes close to her mother's bed.

'You must forgive my intruding, ma'am,' said the old man, with a polite bow; 'but I'm so fond of little folks, and I've brought this little girl of yours a picture, if she will accept it from me.'

A flush of pleasure came into the child's face as he brought out of his pocket his promised gift. She seized it eagerly, and held it up before her with evident delight, while her mother raised herself on her elbow to look at it also.

It was the picture of a shepherd, with a very kind and compassionate face, who was bearing home in his bosom a lost lamb. The lamb's fleece was torn in several places, and there were marks of blood on its back as if it had been roughly used by some cruel beast in a recent struggle.

The shepherd seemed to have suffered more than the lamb, for he was wounded in many places, and his blood was falling in large drops on the ground. Yet he did not seem to mind it; his face was full of love and full of joy as he looked at the lamb.

He had forgotten his sorrow in his joy that the lamb was saved.

In the distance were some of the shepherd's friends, who were coming to meet him, and underneath the picture were these words, printed in large letters:

'Rejoice with Me, for I have found My sheep which was lost. There is joy in the presence of the angels of God over one sinner that repenteth.'

The little girl read the words aloud in a clear, distinct voice; and her mother gazed at the picture with tears in her eyes.

'Those are sweet words, ain't they?' said the old man.

'Yes,' said the woman with a sigh; 'I have heard them many times before.'

'Has the Good Shepherd ever said them of *you*, ma'am? Has He ever called the bright angels together and said to them of *you*, "Rejoice with Me, for I have found My sheep which was lost?'

The woman did not speak; a fit of coughing came on, and the old man stood looking at her with a very pitying expression.

'You are very ill, ma'am, I'm afraid,' he said.

'Yes, very ill,' gasped the woman, bitterly; 'everyone can see that but Augustus!'

'That's my father,' said the little girl.

'No; he doesn't see it,' repeated the woman; 'he thinks I ought to get up and act in the play just as usual. I did try at the last place we went to; but I fainted as soon as my part was over, and I've been in bed ever since.'

'You must be tired of moving about, ma'am,' said the old man compassionately.

'Tired!' said she; I should think I *was* tired; it isn't what I was brought up to. I was brought up to a very different kind of life from *this*,' she said, with a very deep drawn sigh; 'it's a weary time I have of it - a weary time.'

'Are you always on the move, ma'am?' asked the old man.

'All the summertime,' said the woman. 'We get into lodgings for a little time in the winter; and then we let ourselves out to some of the small town theatres; but all the rest of the year we're going from fair to fair - no rest nor comfort, not a bit!'

'Poor thing! Poor thing!' said the old man; and then a choking sensation appeared to have seized him, for he cleared his throat vigorously many times, but seemed unable to say more.

The child climbed on one of the boxes, and brought down a square red pincushion from the shelf which ran round the top of the caravan. From this she took two pins, and fastened the picture on the wooden wall, so that her mother could see it as she was lying in bed.

'It does look pretty there,' said the little girl; 'mummy, you can look at it nicely now!'

'Yes, ma'am,' said the old man, as he prepared to take his leave; 'and as you look at it, think of the Good Shepherd who is seeking you. He wants to find you, and take you up in His arms, and carry you home; and He won't mind the wounds it has cost Him, if you'll only let Him do it. Good day, ma'am,' said the old man; 'I shall, maybe, never see you again; but I would like the Good Shepherd to say these words of you.'

He went carefully down the steps of the caravan, and Rosalie stood at the window, watching him picking his way to the other shows, to which he was carrying the same message of peace. She looked out from between the muslin curtains until he had quite disappeared to a distant part of the field, and then she turned to her mother and said eagerly:

'It's a very pretty picture, isn't it, mummy?'

No answer came from the bed. Rosalie thought her mother was asleep, and crept on tiptoe to her side, fearful of waking her. But her mother's face buried in the pillow on which large tears were falling.

When the little girl sat down by her side, and tried to comfort her by stroking her hand very gently, and saying: 'Mummy dear, mummy dear, don't cry! What's the matter, mummy dear?' her mother only wept the more.

At length her sobs brought on such a violent fit of coughing that Rosalie was much alarmed, and fetched her a mug of water, which was standing on the shelf near the door. By degrees her mother grew calmer, the sobs became less frequent, and to the little girl's joy, she fell asleep. Rosalie sat beside her without moving, lest she should wake her, and kept gazing at her picture till she knew every line of it. And the first thing her mother heard when she awoke from sleep was Rosalie's voice saying softly:

'"Rejoice with Me, for I have found My sheep which was lost. There is joy in the presence of the angels of God over one sinner that repenteth".'

Classic

A Peep Behind
The Scenes

Little Faith

# Fiction

## Christie's Old Organ

## The Basket of Flowers

*Classic*

*Fiction*

## The Basket of Flowers

### *By Christoph Von Schmid*

Mary lives a sheltered, peaceful life in a little cottage with her father. Under her father's watchful gaze Mary learns valuable lessons about faith, purity and forgiveness. All these lessons will come in useful sooner than Mary realises.

The local landowner's daughter, Amelia, is Mary's best friend and Mary gives Amelia a gift of a beautiful basket of flowers for her birthday. In return Amelia gives Mary a lovely new dress and that is when the trouble begins. Amelia's maid, Juliette wanted that dress for herself! Jealousy rears its ugly head and Juliette sees an opportunity to avenge herself on Mary. When Amelia's mother's ring goes missing Juliette immediately plants the blame on Mary. Mary is then accused of the crime and she and her father are both imprisoned for a crime they did not commit. Will Mary's faith in God survive? Watch out for the surprise.

# Classic Fiction

## A Peep Behind The Scenes

**By O F Walton**

Rosalie and her mother are tired of living a life with no home, no security and precious little hope. But Rosalie's father runs a travelling theatre company and the whole family is forced to travel from one town to the next , year in year out. Rosalie's father has no objections but Rosalie's mother remembers a better life, before she was married when she had parents who loved her and a sister to play with. Through her memories Rosalie is introduced to the family she never knew she had. Rosalie and her mother are also introduced to somebody else - The Good Shepherd. They hear for the first time about the God who loves them and wants to rescue them and take them to his own home in Heaven. Rosalie rejoices to hear about a real home in Heaven that is waiting for her but will she finally find this other home that she has heard about - or is it too late? Will God help her find her family as he helped her find him? Of course he will!

*Classic*

*Fiction*

## Christie's Old Organ

### By O F Walton

Christie knows what it is like to be homeless and on the streets - that's why he is overjoyed to be given a roof over his head by Old Treffy, the organ grinder. But Treffy is old and sick and Christie is worried about him. All that Treffy wants is to have peace in his heart and a home of his own. That is what Christie wants too. Christie hears about how Heaven is like 'Home Sweet Home'. Everytime he plays it on Treffy's barrel organ he wonders if he and Treffy can find their way to God's special home. Find out how God uses Christie and the old barrel organ and lots of friends along the way to bring Treffy and Christie to their own 'Home Sweet Home'.

*Look out for further*
*Classic reprints:*
*The Family Devotional*
*Guide to the Bible*

*In the Year 2000:*
*Peep Of Day*
*Line Upon Line 1*
*Line Upon Line 2*

*In the Year 2001*
*More about Jesus*
*Precept Upon Precept*
*Lines Left Out*

## TRAIL BLAZERS

## The Freedom Fighter
## William Wilberforce

by
### Derick Bingham

*'No! No!' cried the little boy, 'Please no! I want to stay with my mother!'*
*'Be quiet!' shouted the man who roughly pulled his mother from him. She was taken to a raised platform and offered for sale, immediately. The heartbroken mother was to be separated from her little boy for the rest of her life...*

This was the fate of thousands of women and children in the days before slavery was abolished. One man fought to bring freedom and relief from the terrors of the slave trade; it took him forty-five years. His name was William Wilberforce. His exciting story shows the amazing effect his faith in Christ and his love for people had on transforming a nation.

'A story deserving to be told to a new generation.'
The Prime Minister the Rt. Hon. Tony Blair, M.P.

ISBN 1-85792-371-5

## From Wales to Westminster
## Martyn Lloyd-Jones

by his grandson
Christopher Catherwood

*'Fire! Fire! - A woman shouted frantically. However, as the villagers desperately organised fire fighting equipment the Lloyd-Jones family slept. They were blissfully ignorant that their family home and livelihood was just about to go up in smoke. Martyn, aged ten, was snug in his bed, but his life was in danger.*

What happened to Martyn? Who rescued him? How did the fire affect him? And why is a book being written about Martyn in the first place? In this book Christopher Catherwood, Martyn's grandson, tells you about the amazing life of his grandfather, Dr. Martyn Lloyd Jones. Find out about the boy who trained to be a doctor at just sixteen years old. Meet the young man who was destined to become the Queen's surgeon and find out why he gave it all up to work for God. Read about Martyn Lloyd-Jones. He was enthusiastic and on fire for God. You will be, too, by the end of this book!

ISBN 1-85792-349-9

## The Watch-maker's Daughter
## Corrie Ten Boom

by
Jean Watson

If you like stories of adventure, courage and faith - then here's one you won't forget. Corrie loved to help others, especially handicapped children. But her happy lifestyle in Holland is shattered when she is sent to a Nazi concentration camp. She suffered hardship and punishment but experienced God's love and help in unbearable situations.

Her amazing story has been told worldwide and has inspired many people. Discover about one of the most outstanding Christian women of the 20th century.

ISBN 1-85792-116-X

# Two New Trailblazers...

## Hudson Taylor
### An Adventure Begins
by Catherine Mackenzie

## George Muller
### The Children's Champion
by Irene Howat

# CHRISTIAN FOCUS

*Good books with the real message of hope!*

Christian Focus Publications publishes biblically accurate books for adults and children.

If you are looking for quality bible teaching for children then we have a wide and excellent range of Bible story books - from board books to teenage fiction, we have it covered.

You can also try our new Bible teaching Syllabus for 3-9 year olds and teaching materials for pre-school children.

These children's books are bright, fun and full of biblical truth, an ideal way to help children discover Jesus Christ for themselves. Our aim is to help children find out about God and get them enthusiastic about reading the Bible, now and later in their lives.

**Find us at our web page: www.christianfocus.com**